Someday a Tree

by EVE BUNTING

Illustrated by RONALD HIMLER

CLARION BOOKS · NEW YORK

Clarion Books
a Houghton Mifflin Company imprint
215 Park Avenue South, New York, NY 10003
Text copyright © 1993 by Eve Bunting
Illustrations copyright © 1993 by Ronald Himler

For information about permission to reproduce selections
from this book, write to Permissions, Houghton Mifflin Company,
215 Park Avenue South, New York, NY 10003.

Printed in the U.S.A.

Library of Congress Cataloging-in-Publication Data
Bunting, Eve, 1928–
Someday a tree / by Eve Bunting ; illustrated by Ronald Himler.
p. cm.
Summary: A young girl, her parents, and their neighbors try
to save an old oak tree that has been poisoned by pollution.
ISBN 0-395-61309-4
[1. Trees—Fiction. 2. Pollution—Fiction.]
I. Himler, Ronald, ill. II. Title.
PZ7.B91527Sm 1993
[E]—dc20
92-24074   CIP   AC

WOZ 10 9 8 7 6 5 4 3 2 1

To Andrea Karlin, who once gave me a tree.
—E.B.

To my brother, my friend, Dr. Thomas Himler.
—R.H.

Every afternoon, when the weather's nice, Mom and I and our
sheepdog, Cinco, walk across Far Meadow and sit under our oak
tree. Dad says the tree may have been here when Columbus came
to America. Mom and I bring lemonade, or pocketsful of our small,
tart apples, and I gather acorns for my collection. Always we bring
biscuits for Cinco and a book for us.

"Once upon a time, in a land far away..." Mom begins.
Cinco lays his head on his paws and listens, too.
Or Mom and I tell stories.
"Tell how, just before I was born, you and Dad stopped here
one day to picnic under the tree and you saw that the land and the
house were for sale..." I stop for breath.
"And we were tired of living in the city and we bought them,"
Mom finishes.
"Tell how I was christened under the tree," I say. "Tell how
a bird did you-know-what on the Reverend's head, and Mrs.
McInerney wore a hat with real flowers on it. And the bees came."
We roll on the grass, laughing, and Cinco rolls and laughs, too.

On hot days people driving from city to city often stop to picnic the way Mom and Dad did. We don't mind. Dad says the tree isn't ours anyway because no one can own a tree. The people spread their blankets and pretend not to be listening to our stories. But sometimes we see them smile.

Today I am doing my favorite thing. I'm lying under our tree, staring up through the leaves. Mom and Cinco are asleep beside me. The clouds change like smoke and the leaves whisper to them as they pass. I think I hear them whisper my name, too.

"Alice...

"Alice..."

Above my head a spider sways. Somewhere an owl lives, hidden. Sometimes, when the dusk thickens, we hear him call and see his pale shadow.

I turn on my stomach and bury my face in the grass. Why does it smell so funny? I sniff.

"Mom?" I sit up. "Mom?"

Her eyes open.

"How come the grass smells like this?" I ask. "Why is it this weird, yellow color?"

Mom yawns. "I expect it's because it has been so hot."

We bring Dad to look. "There's supposed to be rain tonight," he says. "That's probably all the grass needs."

But the rain doesn't help.

Every day that yellow stain spreads. The grass around the tree is withering.

We peer up into the leaves. They are dry and dull and drift down on our upturned faces. It's only spring, but the leaves are falling.

Mom puts her hand on the trunk as though checking for a fever.

Dad kicks at the stiff grass.

"It's as if something was spilled here," he says. "I think we need to call a tree doctor."

When the tree doctor comes, she crumples one of the fallen leaves and scoops a sample of dirt from around the trunk.

"Is the tree very sick?" I whisper.

She touches my cheek. "I need to run some tests before I'll know for sure. Keep thinking good thoughts, honey."

Four days later we find out that our tree has been poisoned.

"But who would do a thing like that?" Mom cries.

Dad's face is grim. "Maybe someone dumped chemicals they weren't supposed to dump. Maybe it was quicker and easier to unload their stuff here by the road."

I don't understand about chemicals. But I know this is bad.

The word about our tree gets around. There's even a picture
of it in the newspaper.

When Mom and Dad and I start to dig the poisoned dirt from
around the trunk, the McInerneys from down the road come to
help. They've brought spades and they work with us, packing in
fresh soil. We hadn't even asked.

The fire department sends tanker trucks to spray water on the faded leaves. By now the top branches are bare, and Dad and Mr. McInerney and Mr. Rodriguez climb up and wrap them in sacking to save them from the sun.

Mrs. Jackson, who works for the telephone company, borrows poles that are as tall as our tree. She and her friends put them up and hang sunscreens between them so our tree is always in the shade.

They hope with us.

But the leaves keep falling.

"Rain has helped to soak the poison in," the tree doctor says. "I don't think your tree has the strength left to fight."

A woman comes with a red scarf she has knitted. It's as long as a jump rope. She ties it around the trunk and pats it in place. "There," she says. "It never hurts to muffle up."

There are get-well cards lined on the grass.
A balloon shaped like a heart floats from a branch.
Someone has brought a bunch of bluebonnets in a jelly jar and
a can of chicken soup.

But still the leaves fall.

The birds have gone. The squirrels, too. Deer used to come at night, tiptoeing down from their secret places. They don't come anymore and the dusk is filled with silence.

"Is our tree dying?" I ask Dad. "Is that why the birds and the animals have gone?"

"The noise around here has spooked them, that's all," Dad says.
I want to believe him but I'm scared. Cinco won't go close to the
tree now either. Each night I watch from my window for the deer.
If the deer come back...but they don't.

One night I'm so unhappy I go to Mom and Dad's room. Their door is open. They don't see me. My mom is crying. Dad has his arms around her.

"A tree lives and a tree dies," Mom says. "But not like this."

Dad strokes her hair. "Shh, sweetheart! The person who did it probably didn't mean to kill the tree. We never mean to kill the beauty in the world. We just do."

I slip away to lie on my bed. My chest hurts so bad. I thought our tree would always be here, like the sky, like the fields, like my mom and dad. I was wrong.

Moonlight whitens my room and I see the big jar of acorns on my dresser. My collection! Some are old, but the ones on top I gathered just a little while ago, when the tree was well. I'm so excited I can hardly breathe.

I leap out of bed and take the acorns on top. In the curl of my hand they seem to be beating, bursting with tree life. I run to the window. I'd go now, but it's dark when the moon slides behind the clouds, and the outside dark still scares me.

I sleep with the acorns in my hand and I'm still clutching them, warm and damp, in the morning.

I race barefoot downstairs.

Cinco is on the porch. He lifts a sleepy head, watches while I get Mom's trowel, and paces beside me as I run across Far Meadow.

It has rained again in the night. The air smells of it. Wet grass and shreds of Indian paintbrush cling to my pajama legs.

The dead leaves from our tree have been raked into piles but others have fallen in the night. I rustle through them. Cinco hangs back.

The tree seems to have shrunk. The top sacking hangs like wet rags. The red scarf, long as a jump rope, is loose. Mrs. Jackson took the borrowed poles back a week ago.

The tree has given up. So have we.

I hold the acorns toward it on the flat of my hand.

"I don't know, Tree," I say. "But maybe."

Cinco helps me pace off giant steps till I'm sure we're on healthy ground. He helps me dig a little trench. I drop the acorns in, one by one, and cover them up.

"Don't you go making plans to come back and dig here again," I tell Cinco. "If even one of these grows, we'll have a tree, big as this!" I spread my arms and stand tall. "Bigger, even."

Cinco cocks his head.

"I don't *know* when," I answer. "Someday."

I stop at the tree to retie the red scarf and pat it the way the woman did. "There you go," I say.

It's strange. There are hardly any leaves left on the tree, but as
Cinco and I are running back to the house I think I hear a rustle
behind us. I think I hear a whisper:

"Alice...

"Alice..."

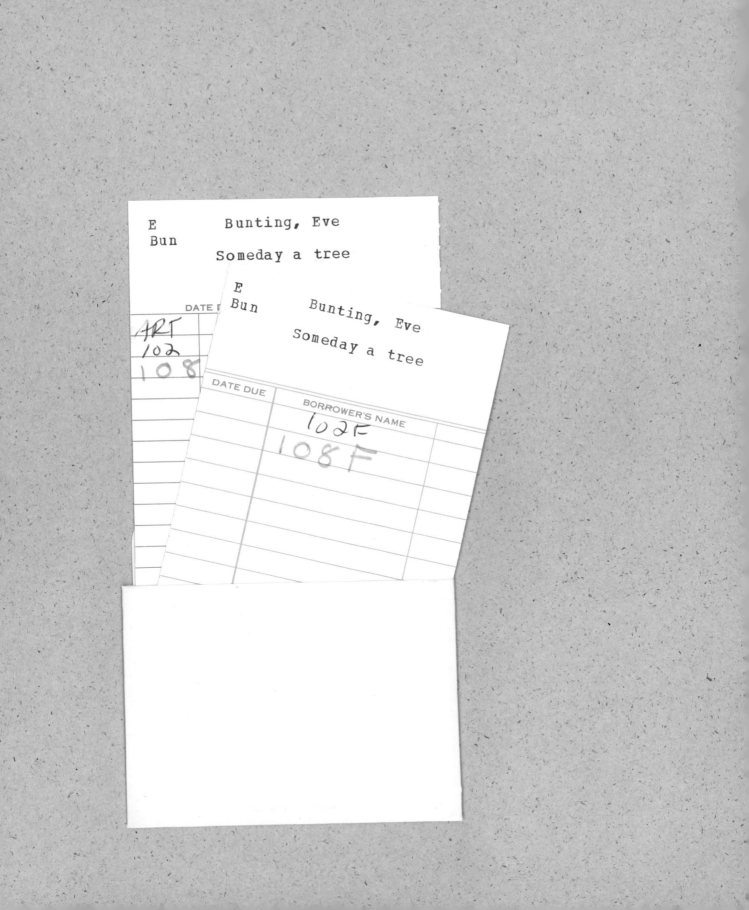

E   Bunting, Eve
Bun

       Someday a tree

E   Bunting, Eve
Bun

      Someday a tree

ART
102
108

DATE DUE	BORROWER'S NAME	
	102F	
	108F	